Title: A Perfect Fit
Subtitle: Billionaire and Gay MM Romance Story

Thank you very much for purchasing this book.

Table of Contents

A Perfect Fit
Description

Cameron Folly spends his days and nights in the ER. His job was the perfect get-away from his lack of a social life, and he enjoyed it more than anything else, till he met the charming Trevor Avery.

The last time Cam was this attracted to anyone, it ended with him left standing alone on his high school prom night dance floor and since then he had kept matters relating to the heart strictly on lock.

He meets Trevor when his sister insists, he follows her to check out the chef she hired for her wedding because she knows he's got great taste in confectioneries and a good eye for colors.

Trevor and Cam hit it off instantly. Their attraction is mutual, and although Cam is a bit too locked up, Trevor knows there's a hidden spark beneath the cool exterior.

Their attraction sparks into something more when they begin to hang out, and Although Cam is having the time of his life, he is just not certain a man as fearless and bold as Trevor is the right fit for him.

When his sister's Christmas Eve wedding ends with disaster brewing and an accident neither of them could have seen coming, Cameron realizes being too careful isn't surest way to preventing heartbreak.

Falling in love with Trevor Avery might be dangerous for him, but still, he might just be the perfect fit.

Chapter 1

"Cameron, make sure you get me those CT scans."

"Sure thing, Doctor Gretchen," Cameron replied as he strode out of the operating room. He took off his scrub caps and massaged the back of his neck with his hands as he stepped on the corridor. After spending three hours standing in front of an open body, he couldn't think of any other way he would prefer to spend his night.

"How are you, Cam?" Hannah, a nurse in the emergency unit replied when she came to stand beside him at the surgical board. His name was displayed over three other surgeries for the next day, and the same happened for the rest of the week. He was always swamped with work, and he loved it that way.

Surgery is his life.

"Tired, but still pumped up," he replied. "It's a night shift, Hannah dear, a lot can happen during night shifts."

"Urggh, you don't need to remind me. Cameron spent the last hour taking out a key from a man's throat. Why would you swallow a key just to make sure your girlfriend doesn't leave the house?"

"The things people do for love," Cameron replied in a singing voice, and they burst into a short round of laughter. Hannah Kennedy was by far his best nurse on in the unit. They had started practice together, and we both third year residents, but Hannah was taking a year back this year to take care of her baby. Cameron's gaze dropped to her already rounding stomach, and he saw her run her right hand over it.

"How's the little one doing in there?"

"He's kicking a lot these days," she replied and offered him a bright smile. "The baby's birth is all Xavier can think about, and we still have about four months left. Cameron wonder what I'll do when the baby finally comes, it's going to be frustrating having him around me all the time."

"I know." He gave her a gentle pat on her shoulder and massaged a little. "Just take it easy anyway and try not to stay for so many night shifts. Don't forget you need rest."

"I have you to always remind me."

Cameron was still smiling as he walked away from Hannah and headed for the resident's on-call room. It was two weeks from Christmas, and this season the emergency unit had most of its cases. It was why he decided to run night shifts for the next few weeks, till the year ran out.

If he was lucky, he could even run a night shift on New Year's Eve. He had nothing better to do anyway. His family always goaded him about not having a social life outside the hospital.

"Name one friend who isn't a doctor, or nurse or medical practitioner of any form," his sister would say and his parents would count the seconds till he came up with a name, but there wasn't ever a name.

He was surrounded by geniuses; was that such a bad thing?

Cameron lowered himself to the bed and few minutes into his rest, his pager beeped again. He jumped to his feet, the three minutes rest enough to get him pumped up for another long hour which was just part of the night.

When he got to the emergency section, he gasped when three nurses rolled the stretcher into the room and pulled curtains around the patient.

"Car accident, thirty-year-old male, his partner is quite hysterical outside, says he ran him down."

"On purpose?" Cameron asked with wide eyes as he slipped his hands into a glove. He began the necessary emergency steps while the nurses checked for a pulse and connected their patient the EKG.

"Possible signs of head trauma, and abdominal distention means he might some internal bleeding. Cameron think we need to open him up," he suggested.

"You're right, Folly," Richard Gretchen, the on-call attending doctor for the night said. "It's the holidays and we're a bit short staffed as always during the night shift, so do you think you can handle this one on your own?"

"Yes, Doctor Gretchen," he replied.

"Great, go save this man's life."

As Cameron rolled the patient towards the operating room unit with the nurses, he saw the smile on Hannah's face as she watched him from the nurses' station. The procedure lasted for one hour, and when he came out of the operating room this time, it was thirty minutes past midnight.

Cameron yawned, and knew he had to get himself a dose of caffeine if he was going to make it through the early hours of the morning. The period of three- five was always the most tiring during a night shift in the emergency unit.

Most of the buzz had died down, and the superiors left the interns in charge till it was time for rounds. Fountain Memorial Lower Manhattan Hospital was a teaching hospital, and a number one trauma center.

Cameron loved the experience he had gotten from here so far, and he planned to continue working here for a long time regardless of his family's suggestions that he take a less tasking career specialty.

He got himself the coffee and ended up taking two cups before the break of dawn. When Cameron finally got off work the next morning, he was sleepy and exhausted, and all he could think off was the hot tub in his bathroom, and his cat.

His phone buzzed when he got to where he parked his black sedan. He took out his phone and answered with looking at the screen properly.

"Hey, sucker," his sister's excited voice boomed into his ear.

Cameron groaned. "Gracie ... you're awfully excited when it's still quite early in the day."

"I know right, and you should be too," she relied, giggling. "Today is the day remember?"

"What? What day?" he asked, not liking where this was going. Whenever Gracie called like this, it always involved him going out of his way to make her happy, especially now because of her wedding preparations.

Why would anyone want to celebrate their wedding on Christmas day anyway, he thought?

"It's his cake tasting day, Cam, and you promised to come with me."

Cameron groaned and slapped a hand over his forehead. "That was today? Gracie ... Cameron just got off a night shift, and—"

"You promised, Cam," she countered and he sensed the sadness in her tone.

"Fine ... all right, I'll meet you, just text me the address."

"Thanks, Cameron, you're the best."

Chapter 2

Cameron rushed into the pastry shop. "Oh, God, Gracie, I'm sorry I'm late," he apologized as he hurried into the shop, and took off the shoulder bag strapped around his shoulder.

"No problem, you're just in time to meet Trevor," Gracie replied, beaming, and Cameron turned to look at the man who stepped out of the adjoining door holding two saucers

"I've brought in the coffee-flavored, and the red-velvet for your tasting, and I'd like to hear thoughts pumpkin," the man said.

Cameron's pulse skittered a bit the minute his eyes landed on Trevor's, and his breath caught in his throat. When his sister mentioned cake tasting, he imagined coming to sit here with an older lady who would lecture them on colors, and cake flavors, but instead he was staring into the most beautiful eyes had ever seen.

Trevor's green eyes sparkled, and Cameron took in the square set of his jaw, high chin, and blonde hair that toppled down to the side of his face. Heat rushed through him, and his pulse started to race when Trevor's gaze slowly trailed over his face too.

Cameron knew when a man was interested in him. He wasn't a middle school kid, but what made him tremble inside was the thought of Trevor being instantly attracted to him that crossed his mind.

Is it even possible that he is? Trevor looked like the bold kind. He had a wide smile, piercings in his left year and a large arm tattoo exposed from the sleeveless top he wore. Cameron on the other hand was always too shy to wear anything but shirt and scrubs. He didn't even think he looked good in any of them. He never had time to gym and build his body, and when he was younger his father always teased by saying he had two daughters.

Trevor held his gaze for a second, his smile unwavering, and he dropped the saucers on the table. "Hi, you must be Cam, Gracie talks about you all the time."

Cameron took his extended hand, and his skin tingled from where their skin touched. Cameron's skin flushed, and he tried to hide it by taking his hand out of Trevor's.

"Nice to meet you, Trevor."

Trevor clapped his hands together. "I really need you to try this. Gracie here is like a little cake whore, no offense. She can't seem to make a decision and it's killing me because the wedding is only a few days away," he said with small hand gestures Cameron already loved.

"Weeks away actually," he interrupted. "And Gracie here is always indecisive with everything. It's why she needs me."

Staring into Trevor's green eyes somehow took away most of the fatigue plaguing Cameron, and he took a seat beside his sister, smiling at her.

"Come on, let me have a taste."

The minute he said the sentence, his eyes widened, and he flushed because it sounded weirdly sexual even to him who was always serious. Gracie laughed, and so did Trevor.

"Don't worry, Cameron know the taste you're referring to," Trevor said, and placed his hand lightly on Cameron's arm.

Was that flirting ... hell it looks like it is.

Cameron did not remember what it was like to flirt with a man. The last time he did anything remotely close to

9

this, he was in senior year, and it ended with him standing alone on the dance floor with no date.

"This is amazing," Cameron said when he tasted the red velvet. "I love it already and ii don't think Cameron want to taste any other thing."

"Try the other one," Gracie said as Trevor lifted a fork to his lips. Cameron accepted the offer, and the cake melted into his tongue the minute he did.

'Oh wow ... it's amazing how you've made coffee taste this wonderful."

"See why Cameron can't make a choice?" Grace asked. "Trevor is just too good at everything."

"You flatter me," Trevor said.

Gracie's phone rang, and she stepped out of the shop after excusing herself. Now that they were alone in the shop, Cameron didn't know what to say.

Trevor stared at him intent, and it made his blood heat up. He shifted in his chair, and tried to start a conversation, but Trevor beat him to it.

"I love your eyes."

Cameron gasped. "Really? Cameron was ... Cameron was going to say the same thing you know," he stammered and ran a hand through his hair. "I should have said it first...."

"It's fine," Trevor said. "I just thought you should know. You must get such compliments often, so it doesn't mean much."

Are you kidding? It means a lot.

Cameron smiled instead. "You know if Gracie can't make a choice, then just give her the best you've got."

"I plan to do that, but ... Cameron can't seem to make a choice myself. so maybe you could help me pair something with red-velvet."

Unable to resist, Cameroon took another taste of the red velvet. "Maybe vanilla or buttermilk. Cameron don't know much about these things, but—" his words died in his throat when Trevor reached out a hand wiped the corner of his lips with his thumb.

"You had a smudge there," he said, and put his thumb in his mouth.

He licked, and the act sent electricity right through Cameron, making it difficult for him to think of anything else but what just happened. His heart thumped wildly in his chest, and he swallowed.

"We can meet up tomorrow to help put her out of her misery, what do you say?"

Cameron blinked and nodded his agreement. "That ... that sounds like an awesome idea," he stuttered.

What is wrong with me, and why can't Cameron form words?

"Good, then it's a date."

Oh ... I'm going on a date.

Gracie came into the shop again and Trevor slid out of his seat. Cameron couldn't help but stare at his backside as he walked away. He turned to Gracie who had a mischievous grin on her face. "So, what do you think of Trevor?"

Chapter 3

Trevor Avery knew he needed more fun in his life. Baking was fun for him, he enjoyed it, and he did because he could. It was why he also invited Cameron, Gracie's brother to hang out with him today.

He spent the entire night staring at the number he got from Cameron before they left his bakery yesterday, and he couldn't stop the smile on his face. The minute he set eyes on Cameron, he knew he wanted to see him again, and the cake tasting was just an excuse.

Gracie had mentioned her brother was gay when they first met, but he never expected that he would be instantly attracted to him, but he was, and Trevor was the man to always go after what he wanted without second thoughts.

He wiped the table he spent hours baking on clean and took off the apron he wore. Cameron should be here any minute, and he wanted to make a good second impression. He stepped out of the kitchen to the dining area and attended to a few customers that walked in before he Cameron finally arrived.

Trevor's heart skipped a beat when he came into the bakery, all smiles, his blue eyes sparkling as they greeted each other with a light hug. He caught a whiff of Cameron's scent when they came closer, and it immediately intoxicated him sending shivers up his spine.

"Hey ... how are you?" Cameron asked when he pulled back and took a seat.

"I'm great and hyped that you could make it."

"Well, as exhausted as Cameron am, Gracie's wedding is important to me. Cameron won't hear the end of it if this event doesn't go as planned. Besides, she's going bridal dress testing today with her girls, and trust me, Cameron can't be a part of that."

Trevor joined in his laugh. "Trust me, Cameron know what it feels like when people assume that you're into that kind of stuff. Cameron mean .... Cameron do love dresses, and Cameron like to play with colors, but do Cameron want to dress like a lady or spend hours in the mall? Definitely no!"

Cameron loved his laughter already. It was like rippling sound waves, and it breezed past him, making him flush.

"So, what do you have for me?"

"I've got white chocolate raspberry cake, coconut and lime, carrot, and pink champagne cake."

"Wow, never heard of the last one, but I'm sure it'll be nice," Cameron said, and rose to his feet when Trevor pulled him up. Trevor led him into the kitchen and showed him the cake already displayed on the table.

He watched Cameron take a bite of each of them, and he enjoyed the look of pleasure on his face as he did. It brought heat to the back of his neck and made it difficult for him to think of anything else but Cameron's lips.

They spent their time after that in the kitchen. Trevor prepared a quick meal he didn't plan for, and they ate together, while Cameron talked about his childhood with Gracie.

"I was an only child, so Cameron didn't know what it was like to grow around a lot of people. When Cameron first came out to his parents, they were accepting, but the kids in school weren't," Trevor confided, remembering his high school days.

It was one of the reasons why he had built his confidence to this level. He made a promise to himself never to let anyone act like they were better than him. From what he could tell about Cameron already, the man was a bit of a fun-loving conservative. He sensed he kept a part of him under tight control, and he didn't know if it had to do with his personality or his kind of job, but he knew he wanted to experience how free Cameron could be.

"You know what, we should spend time together tonight," Trevor suggested when they had emptied the bottle of wine he brought out of his fridge in the kitchen. The cake lay forgotten, and they still hadn't made a decision for Gracie, but he didn't mind. He was enjoying this with Cameron, and he could simply make Gracie something out of the red-velvet and pink champagne flavors later.

"Tonight?" Cameron repeated.

"Yes, trust me, it'll be fun. we could for some sushi, and a comedy pop-up show after."

Cameron's phone rang in his pocket then, and he bolted to his feet as he took it out. His gaze turned apologetic and Trevor gave him a soft nod before he picked the call.

"Yes, this is Doctor Folly," Cameron said. "Right ... I'll be there."

He dropped the call and scratched his eyebrow. "I'm so sorry, Trevor, but Cameron have to get to the hospital now."

He was hurrying out of the kitchen, but he came back and grabbed his keys from the table. "It's an emergency," he said, and was about rushing out again when Trevor stopped him by grabbing his arm.

Trevor brought him closer, and without contemplating, he pressed his lips into Cameron's to have a taste of him. As expected, he tasted like a blend of champagne and raspberry. The taste made his groin tighten, and when Cameron parted his lips, his tongue slipped into his mouth, and he deepened the kiss.

It lasted a minute, and his head swooned with the intensity of the pleasure he derived from it. It was like nothing he had ever felt, and he was certain he wanted more of it.

"I'll call you," Trevor said as he ushered Cameron out of his bakery, and he meant it. He pressed a finger to his lips as he watched Cameron drive away in his car, and his heart fluttered in his chest.

This was a wonderful feeling.

Chapter 4

All Cameron could think of was the kiss even twenty-four hours after it had happened. He sat with his family at dinner table, but he didn't listen to their conversation because he was lost in his world of thoughts.

Trevor was a great listener, noticed when they spent time together the previous day, and at some point, it started to feel like he talked about himself a lot. When the emergency call came in, he had been a bit grateful because all he could imagine was what it would feel like to have Trevor's hand on his skin.

He got his wish in the end, and boy, it was more than he imagined. The silky feel of Trevor's lips would stay with him for a long time, he was certain of it.

"You are glowing," Gracie said, cutting into his thoughts, Cameron blinked and realized everyone on the table was looking at him.

"What? No, no, I'm not ... I'm fine."

"I think Cameron is seeing someone, everyone," Gracie announced with a giggle. "Mom, look at how he's so flushed. I'm the one getting married and I'm not even that red when his fiancé is sitting right next to me."

Josh, Gracie's fiancé nodded in agreement, and Cameron's mother, Sarah grinned at him. "Come on, honey, if you're seeing someone then we'd love to meet him, too."

"Yes, Cam, you should bring him to dinner," his father Jay chipped in. Cameron shook his head and rose to his feet. He knocked his chair over and struggled to bring it back up when it fell backwards.

"Guys, please ... I'm not seeing anyone."

"Really? Then what about Trevor?" Gracie asked.

Cameron gasped, and the sweet laugh on his sister's lips smeared off on everyone else while he tried to hide his embarrassment. He hated being the topic of dinner conversation and his love life just wasn't appropriate.

"Trevor the chef?" his mother asked. "I always liked that guy, and he makes the best pastries in lower Manhattan as far as I'm concerned. Cameron didn't know he was gay though."

"Oh, trust me, Trevor's gay. He's been gay since he was born, and he came out to his parents when he twelve."

"Really?" Everyone gasped, and just like that the topic shifted from Cameron.

Grateful for that, he slipped away from the dining room into the kitchen to wash his hands and get a glass of cold water.

"So, tell me, are you really seeing Trevor?" his sister asked behind him, and he jumped because he didn't even notice when she came into the kitchen.

"Don't sneak up on me like that," he complained and smacked her hand playfully before placing the hand on his chest. "And, no, I'm not seeing Trevor."

"You kidding? You know he's into you, right?"

"No, he's not," Cameron denied, and the memory of their kiss entered his mind again. It made his nerve endings sing with need, and he cleared his throat when Gracie narrowed her intense gaze eon his face.

"So, you're saying you don't like Trevor and you're not attracted to him?"

"I ..."

"That means you like him?" she cut in.

"Let me get a word in, Gracie," he exclaimed.

His sister shot him a teasing smile and put a hand on his arm. "Come on, Cam, Cameron know you. You're his sucker face brother, and Cameron love you that is why Cameron am saying this. You have zero clue on anything about relationships and flirting, all you do is save lives. You are nerd, but you're a hot nerd, and Trevor is kind of into you. Cameron could tell from the minute you two met, so for both our sakes, don't mess this up. I'd hate for things to be weird between me and Trevor. He's a dear friend."

"Eww, you sound like we're the ones getting married."

She shrugged as she walked out of the kitchen. Cameron sighed, and poured myself a glass of water, wishing everything Gracie just said was a lie, but it wasn't.

She was right. Cameron had no idea what relationships were like because he'd had never been in one. If Trevor liked him there was a chance. Because Cameron liked him too.

Right?

Cameron ran a hand through his hair, sucked in a deep breath and made up his mind to do something fun for once. Trevor seemed like the out-going kind of guy unlike Cam's usual timid self, and he could try to enjoy this new brewing attraction.

Without thinking, Cameron took out his phone and sent a text to Trevor.

Hey ... still up for something fun tomorrow night? Cameron can find a way out of his night shift.

It took just a second for his reply to come in.

Sure thing... Cameron know the perfect thing for us to do.... looking forward to it.

He added a love emoji, and seeing it made Cameron's heart swell in his chest. *Oh, sweet lord... what am Cameron doing? What if this is a disaster?*

Cameron had never done anything like that, and just the thought of it was scary. He glanced at his watch, it was almost eight and Cameron was already late for his night shift because he didn't want to miss dinner with the family.

It was the holidays, and Cameron already missed out on a lot of family holidays this year because he always kept busy at the hospital. He went into the living room to greet and say goodbye to everyone before slipping into his coat and grabbing his bag.

Gracie followed him out of the house, and gave him a warm hug in the driveway. "Thanks for taking out time to come to dinner tonight, Cam, it meant a lot."

Sometimes Gracie's sweetness made his heart melt, but that was only when she wasn't being a thorn in his side.

"I love you, Gracie."

"Love you, too, Cam," she said and hugged him tighter. "Invite Trevor to the wedding," she slipped in when she pulled away, and Cameron shook his head.

"You're never going to shut up about him, are you?"

She shook her head and waved at him as he got in his car and drove off.

Chapter 5

Trevor took Cameron skating, and he was surprised to learn Cam didn't know how to skate. He laughed hard till his sides hurt as he watched him struggle to get his balance of the skating shoes, and he assisted him by taking his hand.

"You know, when you said fun, I didn't suspect it to be skating," Cameron said through gritted teeth, his cheeks reddened from his embarrassment. "Oh, Trevor, this is so embarrassing."

"It's not," Trevor assured him, and placed his hands tighter in his. "Just stay close to me, and I'll show you."

He led him through the basics on skating, and since Cam was a natural fast learner, in seconds he was doing it on his own.

Cameron squealed in excitement and pumped his fist in the air, celebrating his victory, and they skated around the area three times before they took a break.

They found a spot to sit in the restaurant area, and Trevor got them some milkshakes. Cameron took a long sip while Trevor watched, admiring the pout of his lips as he licked the milkshake off them.

A tremor raced through him, and he allowed his gaze drop further from Cameron's lips to his chest exposed from the loose buttons on his shirt. His cheeks flamed, and he imagined what it would feel like to run his hands down Cameron's chest.

"I'm actually having fun. More than I have had in a long time."

"Is that because you spend your time in the hospital saving lives?" Trevor asked, and Cameron's sharp smile widened.

"You got me. I'm the least interesting person in his family, and Gracie never stops teasing me about it. The last time I went on a vacation, it was voluntary trip to Africa to help sick kids. his life is somewhat pathetic..."

"It's not," Trevor offered. "I find you quite interesting, and I think you've got a wild streak."

Cameron shook his head. "I sincerely doubt that."

Trevor reached into his pocket and took out a piece of paper. He showed it to Cameron, and Cameron read the flavors out loud.

"Coconut, and lime, with pink champagne flavor for the cakes?"

"I thought it'd be perfect. Your sister loves pink, and her fiancée, Josh eats coconut slices for breakfast. It's a blend of them both."

"I think it's genius," Cameron agreed. "I know she'll love it."

A second of silence passed between them then and all they did was stare at each other. Trevor wanted to know what Cameron was thinking, and at the same time, he wondered how Cam would react if he leaned over the table and kissed him here in front of all these people.

Cameron looked away first and his teeth sank into his bottom lip. It sent Trevor into a frenzied state of need, and he did the one thing he had wanted to do since the night began. He leaned in and kissed him.

Cameron jerked away, and the panicked look on his face was not the reaction he was expecting. Trevor frowned as he watched Cameron look around and wipe a hand over his lip.

"I'm sorry ... I thought ..." Trevor began, trying to launch into an apology, but Cameron stopped him with a wave of his hand.

"No, I'm the one who is sorry," Cameron said and in a split second, he was walking away from Trevor, leaving him speechless, and hurt.

What just happened? was all Trevor could think as he made his way out of the building, got in his car and drove home. He spent the entire night in his suite replaying the events of the night in his head and trying to think about what he could have done wrong.

He liked Cameron a lot, and didn't see the need to hide that, so why did Cameron act the way he did? Was he the kind of man who had a problem with being affectionate in front of so many people?

Trevor picked up his phone with the intent to call Cameron, but he got a text from Grace instead. He had been friends with Gracie since they first met when she came into his bakery to buy some pastries for the first time, and he enjoyed her company.

If he was being honest, he would admit to himself that if he wasn't gay then he would have had a thing for her because she was hot, carefree, and probably the most daring person he had ever met.

Her brother was none of those things. He texted Gracie back with a sad emoji, and they ended up staying up late discussing his failed date with Cameron.

Don't worry, I think Cam likes you too, but he's always too scared to let go and let himself feel.

Had he read the signs wrong, and was Cameron not interested in him like he thought?

Or was this Cameron simply being scared to take a chance like Gracie said?

He couldn't tell, and he couldn't stop thinking about it either.

One thing he was certain of was he liked Cameron a lot, and he wanted to see where this would lead. He believed in taking chances, and he had done so twice already. Even though those relationships never worked out.

Trevor decided he would go find Cameron the next day, and he would tell him the truth about what he wanted ... maybe that way, they could start out on the same page.

Chapter 6

Cameron finished stitching up the little girl with a cut on her forehead, and he watched her swallow the pain meds the nurses brought into the room.

"This will probably scar," he commented, and she brushed the tears in her eyes away with her right hand.

"I know ... I'm a big girl, and I can handle it," she replied to him.

"That's good to know," he replied, and gave her parents standing in a corner a soft nod before leaving the room.

Hannah walked over to him once he stepped out, and from the look on her face, he sensed something was up.

"There's a hot blonde at the nurse's station for you," she said, and Cameron frowned.

"What hot blonde?" he asked as they made it to the section where the nurses station stood. He immediately spotted Trevor standing there, leaning over the counter and when Trevor saw him, the corners of his lips shot up.

Cameron's heart did a slow dive, and for a second, he contemplated turning and running on his heels. He was embarrassed about what he'd done last night, running off like that when Trevor had kissed him, and he knew he owed Trevor an apology.

He had panicked. The first time they kissed he was caught off guard, and he had enjoyed the kiss more than any other kiss he had ever had. It was why it wasn't about to happen again. He panicked because he didn't know what to make of the feelings swirling inside him.

I've never felt this way about a kiss, or any man before.

24

Trevor was still beaming when he got to where he stood and Hannah excused herself so they could talk.

"Now, Cameron know you look good in scrubs," Trevor said in a sultry voice, and the sound sent shivers through Cameron. "How are you? I brought coffee, didn't know which you'd prefer so I came with black and cream."

"Cream please," Cameron replied, thankful for coffee at least. His night shift just ended and he should be heading back home to sleep the day away any minute from now.

"As expected," Trevor replied and handed him a plastic cup.

He took the sip and enjoyed the taste on his tongue. "Trevor ... I want to apologize about yesterday, I didn't mean to run out on you like that, and I just..."

"Panicked?" Trevor supplied, helping him out. Cameron pressed his lips together, and he swirled the contents of his cup. "I get it... this is new territory for you because you've not been in a relationship in a while, and—"

"No, that's not it," Cameron said, cutting Trevor short. The tingle inside him spread as he looked into Trevor's eyes, knowing he had to be plain and honest about what he was feeling.

"I've never been in any relationship. One-night stands, and a few short-lived flings yes, but I've always been too busy for anything else, and you don't strike me like the kind of guy that would want a fling."

"You're right, I'm not that guy," Trevor relied, his deep voice sure as ever. Cameron admired that about him. Everything about his aura exuded confidence, and one did not need to know him in person to know that he was confident in himself.

It's not that Cameron lacked confidence. He was good at his job, and everything he tried to do, but there was just that part of him that could near fit into a crowd.

"I want everything, Cam," Trevor said and reached out to touch his hand. He tried to stop his from trembling, but failed, and Trevor noticed this because he smiled a little. "And it's okay to be vulnerable, but you have to let go and give yourself to experience something beautiful, don't you think?"

"I guess you're right," Cameron said and eased into a laugh. the tension in his shoulders faded a little, and it felt like he could relax.

"Are you ready to get off?" Trevor asked.

"Yes, I was about to."

"Great ... I can show you my house at Carnegie Hill then," he said with a grin.

Cameron took his things and left the hospital with Trevor. The drive to Trevor's house was a brief one, and when they reached the house on Carnegie Hill, Cameron gasped.

He got out of the car and stared at the terrace house in his view. "You live here?"

Trevor shrugged. "I occupy just a suite on the bottom floor, but the entire house is mine yes," he replied.

Cameron's jaw slackened when Trevor took him inside the house, and he admired the architectural style of the building. It had an all-white front, but the inside walls were decorated with expensive natural artwork, and 3d paintings.

The furnishing was simple but elegant. Cameron didn't think he had seen anything finer that the view of the pool he got when he realized the entire bottom floor was made of opaque glass.

He went into the kitchen to admire the back view of the outer porch, and sparse trees scattered around the backyard. Cameron could already imagine himself relaxing under one of them, enjoying the shade its leaves provided.

He had never craved a vacation before, but with a view like this, every human would.

"This place is sick," he commented, and Trevor helped him out of his jacket. "I didn't know you were like ..."

"Rich? I get that a lot," Trevor replied with a laugh. "I inherited most of this from his grandpappy, but I like to keep it all on a low-key. Grandpappy lived here, so when he died, and gave me the estate, I decided to move in, and keep the place alive."

"It's a beautiful home," Cameron complimented and looked around the spacious kitchen again.

When he looked back at Trevor, he saw the fierce look on desire in Trevor's eyes, and his breath hitched in his throat. He didn't know who moved first after that second that they stared at each other, all he knew was that he was in Trevor's arms, and their lips joined in a kiss that brought the flames of their passion to life.

Chapter 7

Trevor wanted to feel every inch of Cameron's skin, and as his fingers worked their way into his hair, he marveled in the hardness of his body. Cameron wasn't a body builder, and he didn't have many toned muscles, but he was solid in the right places and it was enough for Trevor.

He deepened the kiss, angling his head so he could taste him more, and press their bodies together. His body trembled when Cameron's fingers moved down his chest and began undoing his buttons, it felt like he would combust from the pleasure he was feeling.

His shirt came off and he took off Cameron's shirt, lowering his kisses to the side of his neck. His hands moved down the smooth skin of his chest and his fingers skimmed over one nipple, drawing a moan from Cameron's lips.

Trevor pulled back, anting, and their eyes met. "Do you want this?" he asked, his voice hoarse.

Cameron's response was to bring his head down for another kiss, and this time they tumbled towards the couch closest to them in the living room.

Trevor's body touched it first, and cam fell on top of him. Their tongue danced, and Trevor trailed a hand over his back.

Their kisses turned desperate as the rest of their clothes came off, and Trevor's hands moved over the bulge in his pants. He was amazed by Cameron's size, and he imagined what it would feel like in his hands and mouth already. All he wanted to do was taste him and watch the look of pleasure on Cam's face as he gave himself to the pleasure.

Trebor pulled away long enough to change positions so he could carry out his deepest thoughts. His tongue touched the tip of Cam's erection first, then ran his tongue over his full length. He was hot, and hard, everything like Trevor imagined.

The loud groan that escaped Cameron's lips was everything, and it heightened his need. He wanted to pleasure him, so he continued his ministrations, taking time to run his hands and lips over his member till he was bucking his hips from side to side on the couch.

Sensations spread all over his body, and he pumped his hands over Cam's erection till there was a loud cry of release. It wasn't over yet. Cameron came on top of Trevor next, and ran his hands over his chest, taking his time to play with his nipples.

Trevor closed his eyes and gave into the pleasure mounting. He had thought about doing this with Cam since the moment of their first kiss. There was nothing more intoxicating than Cam's woody scent, and the tinge of citrus he smelled from his cologne.

He loved a man that could manage to pull off masculine and innocent at the same time.

His chest throbbed when Cameron made him turn to his side, and trailed kisses down his spine. He wanted release, and he closed his eyes, allowing the sensations wracking through him because he anticipated the promising release at the end.

When Cam's lips encircled his erection, he jerked on the couch, about to burst all over his mouth. His hands gripped the side of the couch as the warmth of Cam's mouth continued stroking his length, and he couldn't handle any more of the pressure building inside him.

He exploded with a loud groan and trembled all over till he had emptied himself out. They lay together after that, snuggling into the loud couch, and Trevor giggled inside when he thought of how he would have to clean the couch later.

For now, he wanted to enjoy the warmth of having Cam close, and he didn't want anything to interrupt. He pressed a kiss into Cam's neck, and Cameron stirred in his arms.

"You know ... you should come for Gracie's wedding," Cameron whispered. "You should come as my date."

Trevor's insides warmed and his heart fluttered in his chest. "I would love that."

Cameron fell asleep in the minutes that followed. His light snore made Trevor laugh, but he didn't mind one bit. He left the couch to fix a quick lunch of mac and cheese so when Cam woke up, he would have something to eat. He knew he was exhausted from his night shift, and he had another round coming up tonight too.

The next week that followed, Cameron and Trevor formed a routine, one that Trevor loved more than anything. Having company in his house was one thing he always enjoyed, and as days passed, Cameron was gradually filling the place, first with his spare scrubs, then a tooth burst in the bathroom, and medical textbooks in the kitchen.

Trevor didn't mind one bit. He enjoyed cooking dinner for them both when Cam wasn't on a night shift and bringing coffee to him at the hospital when he was getting off one. Their routine was perfect, and so was their lives.

It was why Trevor worked up the courage to confess his feeling to Cam one evening after they made love in his hot tub. They lay in bed together, and his hand stroked a path down Cameron's arm.

"You're the most beautiful man I've ever met, Cameron," he said, and Cameron turned to face him. "I think I started to fall in love with you when we first met, and now .... Now all I think of is how I feel about you."

Trevor was grinning, and his heart was racing in his chest, but the blank expression on Cameron's face made him tune down his excitement a bit.

"Move in with me, Cam," he added. "I'm so in love with you, and I want to see where this goes."

"I—" Cam croaked and pulled away. "I think I should go," he said, and slipped out of the bed. "I just remembered I have this thing at the hospital and I should make sure everything goes according to plan," he continued and began putting on his clothes.

Trevor watched him get dressed, and he sighed when Cameron smacked a kiss on his lips and hurried out of the room. He sank into the bed after, trying to manage his hurt feelings.

He had suspected Cam wouldn't handle his confession well, and his first thought was to go after him, but after spending the next few hours alone, he decided not to.

If Cameron wanted him at all, then he needed to make the choice himself.

Chapter 8

A week later, Gracie walked down the aisle with the love of her life, and Cameron had never been more miserable.

Since Trevor's confession a week ago, he hadn't called, and even now as he sat in the front row of the well-decorated layout for Gracie's outdoor park wedding, he felt Trevor's gaze burning into his back from behind.

His sister looked glorious in the white-lace gown she wore. The long sleeves reached her wrists and the dress shaped her petite curves perfectly. Her blonde hair was styled by their mother, and she grinned so hard, Cam suspected her cheeks would hurt.

The priest, read a short sermon, and then gave them room to say their vows. Cameron felt tears sting his eyes as Gracie's eyes searched the crowd and landed on his briefly before she began reciting her vows.

He didn't dare look back because he knew Trevor was right behind him, but when Josh said his vows and slipped the ring onto Gracie's finger, he finally did.

His eyes met Trevor's briefly, and all he could see in his green ones was hurt and despair.

I hurt him with my reaction.

Cameron knew this, but it was difficult for him to accept that Trevor was in love with a man like him. He was nothing like Trevor. He was plain and boring ... he enjoyed his coffee with cream, he was a mess because all he cared about where his medical books, and worse off, he knew nothing about being in love.

But is what I feel for him actually love?

He quickly looked away from Trevor and focused ahead as the priest announced it was time for the couple to kiss.

Everyone cheered, and Cameron rose to his feet to go hug his sister after his parents did the same. As he wrapped his arms around her, he whispered. "I love you, Gracie, and I am so proud of you.'

"I love you, too, Cam," she replied, and kissed his cheeks. "Even though I can see that you screwed up with Trevor."

"I don't know if I can fix this one," he replied.

His cheeks burned at her comment and she hugged him again.

Just then, there was a loud explosion that rocked the ground beneath Cam's feet. He heard the sudden eruption and saw the clouds go up in flames. The force sent him crashing to the ground, with Gracie landing on top of him.

Pain burst through his head as it collided with the floor. All he could hear was the terrified screams of the once excited guests gathered to witness this day.

What is happening? What is ....

Another explosion came, and he heard the terrified voice of someone shouting, "It's a crash ... it's a helicopter crash."

It all happened so fast. He managed to get on his feet, and after checking to make sure Gracie and Josh were all right, he went in search of Trevor.

He inhaled smoke as he looked around, people tried to get on their feet, the blaring sounds of sirens in the distance filled the air, and Cameron's chest burned as his panic pushed through him.

"Trevor?" he yelled on top of his voice without thinking. His blood pumped fiercely through him and pushed back the hair on his forehead away so he could see clearly.

What if something had happened to Trevor? What if he was hurt?

He tried not to think of it as he looked around, staggering on his feet. Cold fingerlike terror raced up his spine, and a lump pushed against his throat making it difficult for him to yell again.

"Trevor?" he yelled, his panicked voice more like a croak this time. His head swooned, and the throb in the side of his temple was intense. He pushed that all away and squinted to see properly through the haziness blurring his vision.

"I'm right here," Trevor said behind him, and Cameron spun around quickly. "I'm safe, and I'm right here."

"Oh..." Cameron swooned and collapsed into his arms. "I feared you got hurt or worse," he said as he felt Trevor's strong arms come around him. Cameron gave into the dizziness closing in on him and the last thing he heard was Trevor's panicked scream this time.

The next time he opened his eyes, he saw three pairs of wide eyes staring down at him. Cameron groaned and spoke in a cracked voice. "Am I in heaven?"

"Not a chance, sucker," Gracie replied, and broke into a loud sob. She dropped her head on the side of the bed and began to cry while his mother and father both sat near him on opposite sides.

"We feared you were terribly hurt," his mother said softly, "but the doctor's said it's a concussion and you will be fine."

"Oh … thank goodness," he gasped and closed his eyes again. He swallowed and extended a hand to touch Gracie.

"I thought you died on my wedding day. It would have really sucked," she said and managed a relieved laugh.

The door opened, and Josh came in. He had a band aid on his forehead, and a cast on his arm, but he looked fine overall.

"Everyone is all right?" Cameron asked, and his mother's nod made him sigh in relief.

"No one got hurt except the ones involved in the helicopter crash. What a tragedy … it's probably all over the news already."

Cameron's father put his arms around his wife as she spoke, and Cameron relaxed deeper into the softness of the bed.

His mind went to Trevor, and the terror he felt after the explosion. Cameron shot up on the bed. "Has anyone seen Trevor?"

"No," Gracie replied and moved aside as he struggled to get out of bed. "Where are you going? The doctor's say you need to rest."

"I know … I love you all for worrying about me, but I…I have to find Trevor. There's something I have to tell him."

Gracie gave him a knowing smile and replied. "Go get him."

Chapter 9

Trevor stood outside the hospital and adjusted the lapel of his tux before sucking a deep breath. What a day it had been.

First off, he didn't think he could make it to the wedding and sit behind Cameron knowing fully well that he was yet to get over his feelings for him, and when he saw Cameron come arrive at the park with his family, he had felt a pang of jealousy.

Cameron seemed like the kind of man who would love and appreciate his family, so why couldn't let Trevor in? Why couldn't he take a chance on their growing relationship?

Trevor had decided to put Cameron out of his mind when they stayed three days without speaking. He had poured out his heart to Cameron, and he what did he get in return?

The wedding ended in disaster, and although Trevor felt sorry for Gracie because her special day had been ruined, he didn't want to spend so much time watching Cameron.

He was staying away for his own benefit. For his heart … he had to keep his cool, and let Cameron decide what he wanted to do. So far, Cameron's decision was not in his favor.

Trevor ran a hand over his face and began walking around the hospital's parking lot to get to his car. After the crash, he drove down to the hospital to make sure Cameron was all right.

The doctors that tended to him confirmed he passed out from the shock. The scans showed no serious injury. The news was relieving to Trevor, and now he was certain Cameron would be fine, he had to get out of here.

He opened his car door and was about stepping in when he heard Cameron call for him. Trevor spun around on his heels, and his heart did a slow dive.

Cameron stopped in front of him, panting, and he couldn't bring himself to look away from him.

"Trevor ..."

"Cameron..." they chorused, and Trevor pressed his lips together, maintaining his cool to give Cameron a chance to speak.

"I'm sorry," Cameron launched right in. "You poured out your heart, and I..." He shook his head. "I thought it was too good to be true. Why would a man like you love a man like me?

"I actually do love you," Trevor responded. "What's not to love about you?"

"I just .... I don't know how to do this, and I was scared. Scared that if I let myself love you, then one day you'd leave.... Or maybe you'd soon realize that I'm not worth it. I just .... I don't want to get hurt, and I've never put myself in the position to try anything new before. It's always been easy and no-string attached for me."

Trevor's heart slammed inside his chest. It was all he'd ever wanted to hear.

"But then I met you, and everything changed. When that helicopter crashed right there in front of us, all I could think about was what if I had lost you... I don't want to ever feel that panic again, Trevor. It scares me more than taking a change on this so I guess what I'm saying is, I want to be with you... if you'll still have me."

Trevor saw Cameron's shoulders slump, and he released a huge sigh when he ended his sentence. "Whoa, that was a lot," Trevor said, a smile crinkling up on his lips.

"I do... I just, I had to tell you. I love you Trevor, and I want to see where this leads because not being with you hurts more. This past week has been hell, and I don't want to go back there."

"I missed you a lot to," Trevor admitted and took a step forward. He felt the pressure in his chest ease a bit, and the familiar heat that pumped through him returned just from looking at the bright smile on Cameron's face.

"I guess it's a good thing that helicopter crashed right? I mean, I feel sorry for the victims, but it helped you climb through one hurdle."

Trevor went in for a hug, and he kept his chin on Cameron's head for a second, inhaling his scent before he pulled back and pressed a kiss to his lips.

"Let' go back inside and not keep everyone worried," Cameron said, and laughed. "My sister almost died for a second when I tried to get out of bed, but when I told her I had to find you, she gave me her support."

"I know. Your sister is my biggest fan," Trevor teased and hooked his hand around Cameron's waist. "Are you hurt? How do you feel?"

"Better now," Cameron replied and rested his head on Trevor's shoulder as they re-entered into the hospital building.

As they made their way back to the room where Cameron was a few minutes ago, Trevor caught the shocked look on the faces around them.

"You know if you feel better then maybe we should do something fun this weekend."

"I'm for it," Cameron replied without hesitating, and kissed Trevor on the lips. "Lett me introduce you to his family," he added, then pushed the door open so they could enter, and meet everyone inside waiting for Cameron's return.

Epilogue

A year later... New Year's Eve.

"You're not spending New Year's Eve in the hospital this year remember? You've got me, and our beautiful Lily to come home too," Trevor reminded him over the phone as Cameron slipped out of his stained scrubs and walked into the shower.

"I'll call you, Trevor, I need to wash this slime off me," he said and ended the call.

Minutes later, he smelled clean, and felt fresher than he had in the last 24 hours. He had moved from one operating room to another emergency call, and now he was exhausted.

This was his last night shift for the year. Today was New Year's Eve, and he looked forward to spending it with Trevor, and his cat Lily. They had made plans for the night. Dinner on Trevor's back porch where they had an amazing view of the sky, and Cameron even planned to propose that night.

The year had changed him. He now looked forward to doing the things he'd rarely cared about in the past. He cooked, spent time with Trevor and outings, and this summer he even took a non-work-related vacation to see Trevor's parents in Oklahoma. It was an amazing week, and he learned a lot about the man he loved.

His phone buzzed in his scrub pants again as he stepped out of the locker room and headed for the main unit. Hannah, his friend, came out of elevator, and she beamed the minute she saw him, joining his strides so they walked into the unit together.

"How is your first day back going?" he asked. Hannah had returned from her eight-month maternity leave today and she was excited to get back to work. Cameron admired her agility. He was aware of how difficult it would be for her to keep up with work and care for her baby in the hospital's day care unit. It was a good thing the hospital had one for women like her who wanted to pursue both the dream of being a mother, and a career.

"It hasn't sucked so far, so I'm good."

The blast of sirens the minute her sentence ended tore a laugh from them both. Cameron winked at her as he started tying his scrub caps. "Well, looks like things just got pretty interesting."

"Tell me about it," Hannah replied, and they got to work.

They spent the rest of the shift tending to patients brought in by the ambulances, and three hours to ten am the morning of New Year's Eve, Cameron signed off work to go spend the rest of the day with his family.

Soon, it would be more than just him and Trevor and he had to get used to delegating some work now, so when they finally got a child, he could help Trevor out with parenting.

Yes, they had plans to get a baby. They had talked about it a few times, and Trevor was totally on-board with the idea. Cameron couldn't wait till his residency year was over so they could move into their new phase of their live together.

Trevor had an elaborate lunch already planned for them in the house, and Cameron had no idea his family were invited till they showed up to surprise him.

They enjoyed a conversation about each other's successes over the year and the crazy times Cameron had at work. Gracie and Josh seemed every bit in love as they were on the first day of their marriage, and cam's parents also seemed genuinely.

Cameron felt like the luckiest person amongst them because he had found his number one source of joy when he least expected it. His only sadness that night was that Trevor's parents didn't make it for New Year's Eve this year. Over the past year, he had spoken to them over the phone countless times, and he got along with them just fine.

"This is an amazing dinner, Trevor," he whispered to Trevor after they had finished eating the creamy lemon chicken piccata Trevor prepared for dinner. "I love you."

"I love you too," Trevor replied and rose to his feet. Everyone around the table gave him his attention, and Cameron gasped when Trevor took out a box from the pocket of his shirt and went down on one knee.

Gracie squealed from where she sat, and Cameron's cheeks flamed when his parents chorused. "Aww..."

"Cameron Folly, I love you, and I want to spend the rest of his life doing just that. I think we're meant to be, so what do you say?"

It was a simple sentence, and it made Cameron's heart flutter. Warmth and love for Trevor spread through hm, and he couldn't imagine himself with anyone else for the rest of his life.

He stood up, and helped Trevor to his feet, then did the same thing Trevor did, going down on one knee.

"I can't imagine spending his life with anyone else as his partner, and that's why I also planned this for tonight," he said and took out his ring.

Trevor's smile reached his eyes, and he nodded, extending his hand to Cameron so he could help him get on his feet too. "Of course, I'll spend the rest of his life with you," he replied.

"Let's make a toast," Cameron's father said and joined them on his feet. "To this happy couple, and many more years of joy for them. To Cam and Trevor."

"To Cam and Trevor," everyone chorused just seconds before midnight.

The alarm Trevor had set in their living room alerted them when it was the stroke of midnight, and they made another toast.

"Happy New Year," they shouted in merriment and continued the night. Cameron hoped that their many days ahead was full of joy and hope like this, and he couldn't wait to start this new perfect journey of life with his partner.

THE END

Printed in Great Britain
by Amazon

10402409R00025